T0130525

GORI

REVENGE OF A SAMURAI

James Chaliz

Order this book online at www.trafford.com
or email orders@trafford.com

Most Trafford titles are also available at major online book retailers.

Printed in the United States of America.

ISBN: 978-1-4269-5362-0 (sc)
ISBN: 978-1-4269-5363-7 (hc)
ISBN: 978-1-4269-5364-4 (e)

Library of Congress Control Number: 2010919496

Trafford rev. 03/16/2011

 www.trafford.com

North America & international
toll-free: 1 888 232 4444 (USA & Canada)
phone: 250 383 6864 ♦ fax: 812 355 4082

About Author

I was born in 1961 and was raised in the east side of New York City.

The East River Project the heart of Spanish Harlem. We moved from 105ᵗʰstreet to 103ʳᵈstreet. still in the same projects. I was a small skinny kid, and always got bulled. I was so scared. I was afraid to even cross the streets.

Then at the age of eleven I began to study martial arts. That was the turning point of my life. As I got older my confident grew: and as I gained more knowledge. I began to study on my own and created my own style called (The C-System ----The Art of Change.)

All of the knowledge I have in martial arts, is because of an old friend of mine name (John Flores). And to all of my Sensi's though out my years. Thanks you to all. And to all the readers and critics in this world. I will tell you this; I am not an expert in Japanese culture.

Nor have I studied under any Japanese Literature or under any Author or Teachers. Ever since I was a young boy. I always loved the Japanese way of life, their dedication, loyalty and Honor. for life and for death.

I know in today's world, times are different, but you can still See there traditional ways, that were past down from generations.

I love to write, but I am not a professional" and to tell you the truth" I wrote this story; pretty much, out of nothing. I had a small idea, picked up a pen and began writing. Two years later, I ended up with this,

Gori: Revenge of the Samurai.
I fell in love with these characters the moment my pen touched the paper, yes; paper; its easier to walk around with paper and pen then a laptop. I am now working on the continuation. I hope everyone who reads this story,

Falls in love with the characters the same way I have.

So from me to you, Thank You and enjoy.
J.C

Acknowledgments

First I would like to thank the heavens, without faith we can't envision and release ours creations.

Secondly all my Thank goes out to my Family. To My Wife (Liz) for always standing by my side and putting up with me. love you baby.

To My son (James. A), one of the best writers and film markers I have created. And I'm not just saying that because he's my son; well may be a little, but when his stuff comes out, pick it up, he's twisted. Thanks for keeping me up to date. C.y.

And My Daughter (Mielin. R) My little fashion diva. Thanks for helping me spend money I didn't even have. If I needed something, too help me, she'll tell me to buy it, as long as I buy her something, so she won't rat me out. She keep it up, she will be a millionaire, before she hits thirteen. But she keeps me going, love you Ms. Diva.

To My Mother (Violet), love you always Ma, for alway finding a way to put food on the table, and making something out of nothing.
And to My Brothers and Sisters; for some reason, always looking up to me, peace and love to all.

To Joey and Every one at Inwood Boxing Gym. keep on punching.

Thanks to my best friends (Matt) for all of your help through out the years. I haven't forgotten. And (Doc the Technician) also an Author himself. Love you guys.

A big thanks to Rebecca Crystal a New York City School Teacher, for reading over my material and giving me great pointers and that great teacher's advice that will always be engraved in my head forever. To every one in Crothall and Westchester Medical Center thanks for all of your support.

And a very special Thanks to Rosie Dampios at Trafford Publishing for going out her way and helping me. I truly appreciate your effort in getting this done.

GORI

THE REVENGE OF A SAMURAI

CONTENTS

Main Characters

1) **Yoshima Gorisaki:** Ex Assassin, Mercenarily and Farmer. The Son of Lingho, Husband to Nijei and father to Tomo, Ushi and Yeishi.

2) **Yoshima Lingho:** A Master Sword Smith and Bushido Master, and Husband to Shiyin, father to Gori.

3) **Osamaruko Shiyin:** A beloved wife to Lingho and mother to Gori.

4) **Nijei:** The daughter of Tanglu. The wife of Yoshima Gori and the mother of Tomo, Ushi and Yeishi.

5) **Tenchu:** The young Emperor.

6) **Lutao:** The Shogun and the older brother of Takamuri.

7) **Takamuri:** The Daimyo and the younger brother of Lutao.

8) **Tanglu:** The father of Nijei.

Scene 1
The Revenge of a Samurai

In the 16th century Japan the Emperor was considered by all to be the divine ruler, but the Samurai, was feared by all. The Samurai Warrior formed a class of professionals who governed Japan, under the reign of the highest Samurai called the Shogun, who is held the supreme authority and who is the leader of the Samurai class. The Shogun imposed new laws given by the Emperor. To over see the Emperors orders brings dishonor and disgrace to the Emperor and his imperial palace, and to do so, is to be sentence to death, by his own hands or the hands of another. But there was one, who broke the code of the Samurai.

HERE IS WHERE THE STORY BEGINS..............

It is a beautiful day somewhere in Omi Japan, the sky is bright blue and the clouds are so thick, it look's as if someone had placed them there. From the South, a cool breeze coming from the mountain air, far away from the horizon. Somewhere in a small village lived a farmer named Yoshima Gorisaki. He is working out on the fields, as he stops for a moment to breathe in some of the cool air that is sent from the heavens. He breathes in and looks up to see his family near his home. He smiles with love and relaxation. Yoshima has a wife and three kids; the youngest one is six month old Yeishi, sitting on the ground next to her mother as she is washing laundry by hand and there two boys, six and four, Tomo and Ushi as they play together and getting in the way of every thing and his beautiful wife Nijei. She turns to him, feeling his presence as she is draping the wet clothes over the clothing line. She smiles and waves, Gori waves back and goes back to work on his estate as he is planting his crop to grow rice, fruit, vegetables and herbs for his family, and to auction off for clothing and to pay taxes on the land. On that beautiful morning his life was about to change for the second time in his life.

GORI IN THE FIELD

At that moment, five of the emperor's top soldiers are arriving unannounced, and in the middle of these mighty warriors is the shogun. Wearing a dark red armor with a dragon face mask, right behind him is his brother second in command, the Daimyo Takamuri, dressed in a dark blue armor, his helmet displays a long demon horns, and as usual the lower class foot soldiers wore black. Tomo see them coming up the road and calls out to his father: "Papa! Papa someone is coming!" His mother turns to him and said with a smile: "He can't hear you, he's too far away." Gori is about a quarter of a mile out in the field. Now the soldiers are getting close; Tomo taps his brother Ushi on his shoulder and said: "Let's call out to papa together." Ushi with excitement replies: "Okay" together they both yell: "Papa! Papa! Someone is coming up the road! Papa! " The soldiers are getting closer. Nijei not knowing who's was coming, calmly said to the boys: "Ring the bell that always works." Ushi with excitement said: "Yeah" and picks up a wooden stick and tries to hit the bell. But he could not reach it, he is to short. So Tomo came over and tries to pick him up, but little Ushi was too heavy for him. So Tomo drags a wooden crate over and helps Ushi on top. Tomo asks Ushi: "Is that better?" Ushi anxious to hit the bell replies: Yeah!" and starts hitting the bell as hard as he could. Gori turns and looks up with a smile, but his smile quickly fades as he sees the five horsemen arriving in front of his home. He inhales a deep breath of panic, knowing what was next to come. No, he said to himself as he tightly grippes the handle of the chopping knife, that he uses when working out on the field, and starts to run to his family.

THE SOLDIERS ARRIVING

The shogun with the look of death in his eyes gets off their horses with two of his soldiers. They approached Nijei as she is surprised and shock to see them. The two soldiers walk up and stand in front of her, as they block her view. The shogun himself walks around her without saying a word as he deeply staring menacingly at her. She watched him pass in fear. Standing scared and afraid she picks up Yeishi off the ground and didn't notice her husband as he running towards her. Her two boys are so excited to see them that Nijei had to control them; she nervously by with force tells them: "Hay you two, stand still and show some respect." It was the first time they have ever seen a real samurai, the closest they ever got was the stories their father always tells them at bed time. Meanwhile Gori is still running as fast as he can, but the soil was so soft, it felt like he was running on quick sand. NIJEI! RUN! RUN!!!! She did not hear him, but with every step that Gori takes, he is getting closer.

A breeze softly blows though Nijei's hair as she slightly hears from a faraway distance: "RUN!!! NIJEI!!! RUN!!!" She slowly moves her head and looks over the shoulder of one of the men, and sees her husband desperately running towards her. At that moment the Shogun walks over to the right side of her, and with those dark evil eyes he turns and looks at Gori.

LUTAO THE SHOGUN

Gori is still running from a far distant, see's the shogun as he grabs the handle of his sword with his left hand, and without turning his head, still looking at Gori trying his best to save his wife, grins as he quickly swings his left arm outward. The blade swiftly cuts through the air as it make's a beautiful sound. "Ching" as the blade vibrates; he then puts the blade back into his scabel (case). Nijei's eyes open wide with the look of fear, looking at her husband still running, as he begins to fades away. Gori stops to see Nijei's head fall from her body.

SHOGUN MOVES HIS SWORD ACROSS NIJEI'S NECK

He yells: "NOOOO!!!" as her body falls to the ground, still holding Yeishi in her arms. The Shogun turns and gives an order to his men as he walks to his horse: "Kill them. Kill them all." He then sat on his horse and rode off with his second in command. Gori knows what's to come and begins to run even faster, to try and save his kids. Tomo quickly grabs Ushi's arm and starts to run, and hide in the forest. But as they were nearing the forest, a soldier, still sitting on his horse, sees them. He stares as he jokes to the others: "There they go, trying to hide like two rats." They all start laughing, as the two boys were nearing the entrance of the forest. The soldier quickly pulls out his bow and arrows and take's aim. Tomo looks at Ushi with a smile as they are feeling safe. Seconds later, there's a sound that is quickly cutting thought the air, suddenly they both fell to the ground as two arrows pierces through their backs. Gori is near, about 100 yards away, as he sees what just happened to his two boys. Without stopping, he continues to run even harder as he try's to save Yeishi. One of the foot soldiers walked over and stood over Nijei's body; one of her arms is wrapped over Yeishi. He then take's his sword and aim's it at her as he looks at Gori. He grins at him then quickly shoves his blade downward, piercing through Yeishi's heart and his blade cuts into the ground. Gori is only ten feet away as he stops and stares at the nightmare around him.

His wife headless body, as she lies on the ground, still holding onto his baby daughter with a sword through her chest as the blood continues to run from there body. And near the forest, his two boys as they are lying face down with an arrow through their backs. Then he hears a chuckle coming from the soldier's as one of them said: "You can only hide from us for so long Yoshima." Gori's eyes turns red with rage, he focus in on the three soldiers, at that moment he raises his knife and charges at them, as he lets out a loud yell: "AAAA!!!..."

The three soldiers closed in and formed a diamond shape stance. Gori full of anger swings his knife at the soldier that is standing in the middle. The soldier moves in and blocks Gori's attack with his sword, as the other two moves behind Yoshima from the side, and surrounds him. The air is now getting warmer and Gori is breathing heavier as the air thickens. He is now surrounded, standing in the center of these warriors, his knife facing downward into the muddy ground. Everything slows down in Gori's mind. He see's there is one soldier standing to his right; the other is to his left and the third soldier is standing behind him, and all are ready to attack. The soldier behind him said: "You've seen what we did to your family, now your next!" Gori ask: "Why, Why my family?" The soldier to his left replies: "You betrayed the emperor. You out of all should know not to betray him, no one betrays him. So you and all that belongs to you must die. These are the orders of the Emperors and we will carry them out." Gori eyes fills with tears of anger, stares deeply with hatred, and said: "Today you will be the one's who will die and next will be your precious emperor. I will not rest until you and everyone else are dead."

The soldiers looked at each other with surprise of what their ears had just heard, and then they looked at Gori. The soldier to his right said: "You know when some one dishonors the emperor no one lives, not even you!" GORI grips his knife and replies: "Dishonor, you are not a true samurai, you are barbarians, and if I die, I will not die alone on this battle field." Gori slowly gets into a wide stance, with the blade of his knife facing downward. He closes his eyes for just a moment and takes a deep breath and focuses his energy. At that moment the soldiers charged at him. Gori feels there foot steps as they are getting closer and their breathing getting louder, and within seconds it began. The first soldier yells as he comes with an overhead strike from Gori's left. Gori opens his eyes as he sees the blade coming down, and blocks the on coming attack with an outward block, forcing the energy of the blade to go another direction. Gori quickly steps forward, thrusting his knife into the soldier's chest; as the second soldier comes from Gori's right, with a wide strike to his body, and the third soldier attacking with an angle overhead strike from behind.

Blood spray's every were as Gori pulls his knife out from the chest of the dying soldier, then steps back with his left foot pivoting one hundred and eighty degrees, and in one quick motion he decapitates the head of the soldier that is coming from his right, with his own one handed outward strike, with his right hand. The last man standing is approaching from behind as he is raising his sword over his head. Gori see's him from the corner of his right eye as he continues to move and in two motions, Gori swings his right arm low, slicing the soldier around his stomach, with an outward striking motion. The soldier stops and grabs his stomach to stop his guts from falling out. Gori continues to move with the same momentum, as he swings his knife over and around his head, grabbing the handle with his left hands, and comes downward with all his might. "AAAA!!!!" As Gori plunges the blade of the knife right between the shoulder and neck of his attacker, before he even touches the ground with the first strike. Gori breathing heavy, slightly steps back to watch as his victim slowly went down. Looking into his eyes as he watches as the man's life and soul dissolves from his body.

In his mind everything seems like an eternity, but just seconds had pass as Gori drops to his knees near Nijei and Yieshi's bodies. The sky seems gray and the ground is covered with blood. Gori still filled with anger and rage screams into the air, his whole meaning for life has been snatched from him in one afternoon. Then he breaks down and cries. He looks over to where his two boys lie and lets out another scream of rage.

He walks over to their bodies and picks them up. He hugs them as he carries them over and laid them near there mother. He slowly walks inside his home and pulls out a beautiful white silk sheet, his wife had been working on, and places it over their bodies. On the side of his home is where he keeps his tools, he walks over and picks up the shaberu and begins to dig. Hours pass as dawn grew near. Gori sees the light coming from the horizon. He stops digging as the grave is now deep enough. He walks over to their bodies and pulls the sheet off. He stares at them for a moment, and then he carries Nijei's body into the hole and places her head in the proper position over her body. He then carries Yeishi into the grave and place her in her mother's arms. More tears falls from his eyes as he is having flashes of them being together. Suddenly he snaps out of it, knowing he must continue his task. He then places Tomo and Ushi beside her. He walks over and picks up the sheet, grabs it with both hands and tears off a piece, and puts the piece inside his keikogi. He then takes the sheet and spreads it over the bodies. Gori is so exhausted he could barely climb out the hole. He looks up to the heavens as the day light begins to shine on the dark sky and the night birds flew over head as he wonders to him self: "I have nothing left, but I know deep inside, I must keep going. I can't leave my family out in the open to be found and eaten by the animals that lives in the forest. This is not the end. Once Lutao gets word that his soldiers are missing, he will return with even more men. So I cannot stop. I will not stop." He tosses the shaberu out and grabs the soil with his hands and pulls his way up. He climbs and drags his way out, then turns around on all fours and kneels over the grave sight. He bow's his head and make's a promise: "To my family, before I die and even in the moment of my death, I will avenge yours. No matter what it takes they are all dead. Soon you and I will be together again, but not yet. For now, you rest, as for me, I rest when my promise to you, my loving family is fulfilled." He then picks up the shaberu and begins to cover the grave with its own dirt.

The morning sun begins to rise, as the night sky blends from black to a bright blue. Gori had just finished covering the grave. He puts no marking and left no stones, he just sprinkles some seeds from a small pouch he carries over the grave and said a prayer: "With your death, you will give life. You will be one with nature. The flowers that grow will feed the birds and the lotus tree that rises will give life to all that surrounds you. If I return, this will be my resting place. But for now I must leave you, and finish this." Gori then turns and looks at the soldier's bodies as it lays there. Still exhausted, but with every bit of energy he had left, he drags their bodies over and places them on top of each other. He piles some wood and leaves over the bodies and lights them on fire with two stones. But not before taking the armor off of one of the dead soldiers. As the fire begins to burn, Gori goes into his home and in a secret hiding place; he pulls out something long, wrapped in a dusty cloth. He uncovers it, and unravels a sword. It is a shiny red and black samurai sword and the handle is shaped like a dragons head. This sword his father had in his hands, the moment of his death. On the side of the blade, in Japanese letters it read: "The Yoshima Warrior. We live and die by the code" He covers it up and straps it to his back and begins to walk out the door. He stops for a moment and stares at the horrific scene. He pans his head to his left, to where his family rest. Tears of sadness fills his eye, then he pans to his right, where the fire burns, and the rage once again raises as his eyes turns from sadness to anger. Gori's home felt empty, dry dirt covered with blood and the smell of death flows though the air. He walks out and see something to the far left of his home. There remaining, stand three horses. He pulls two of them out and smacks them on the rear, and send's them running off. The last one is a shiny black stallion which he keeps. He packs the horse with what ever he had, a set of swords The Katana and Wakizashi and the armor he had taken. Gori put's the long sword on the left side of the horse saddle and the short sword he wore on the left side of his hip. He grabs the horses strap and forces himself on saddle. He slowly pans his head around and takes one more look at what once his home. He sees the images of his family. He sees his son's playing together and his wife mending with his daughter. He takes a deep breath as he sighs and said to himself: "In time we will be together." And slowly rides off vanishing into the mountains.

GORI HOLDING CHILD

Scene 2
Lutao and the Emperor

Early that morning, on the north side of the village, and from the south window of the emperor palace, The Shogun (Lutao) sees smoke rising into the sky from a faraway distance, which is miles away from the palace walls. And with satisfaction he said to himself: "The deed is done. Now I must inform the emperor." The shogun grabs his sword and straps it between his hip and beltline, he then turns and grabs his helmet that is resting on a wooden chest, and walks out his chamber. He walks down the steps and through the corridor that leads into a beautiful garden with sandy color pebbles and beautiful flowers. In the middle of the garden there's a manmade waterfall, that sit's ten feet high and a water stream that leads into a small pound, that is filled with authentic fishes from all parts of Japan. In the center of this elaborate garden, sit's the emperor as he is enjoying his beautiful garden and the sky above as he's Meditate.

The shogun walks up to the Emperor and bows his head and said: "My lord, your orders has been fulfilled." The Emperor still sitting at a meditating position replies:

"Good, very good. It has been seven years, since this began, and now it over. Like I said many times, no one betrays me, no one. Never in the history of my ancestors has anyone gotten away with treason or dishonoring the imperial place and it won't begin here, as long as I'm emperor." There a silent pause in the air, as the emperor slowly opens his eyes and looks at Lutao and asks: "Now, are you sure Gori and his family are dead?" Lutao looks up at the emperor without a word. The Emperor continues to say: "This is the one thing you must understand Lutao, Gori was one of my best assassins." Lutao put his head down to show respect. The emperor continues: "Yes... even better than you, Lutao." Lutao slowly looks up to agree with his words, but not willingly. The Emperor then asks him: "Has your soldiers reported in?" Lutao quickly response with confidants: "No my lord, but I left three of my best soldiers behind, and they have signaled me with the code." The Emperor wonders as he asks him: "The Code?" Lutao: "Yes my lord the code. The code of smoke means the mission was a success." The Emperor points to Lutao and said: "How would you know that they lit the fire? If I were you, I'll make sure. Take more men with you this time. And if he's alive, make sure he's dead, bring me his head" Lutao bows his head as he answers: "Yes my lord." The Emperor calmly inhales as he closes his eyes and said to Lutao: "If not, we are in for a war." Lutao stood up as he fixes his armor and replies: "But my lord, he is only one man and we have thousands."

The Emperor slowly opens his eyes and looks at Lutao as he answers: "A thousands soldiers are not enough to defeat this man. We need more than two armies." Lutao is still trying to convince himself as he replies back: "This man? He is nothing but a farmer." With slight frustration the Emperor said: "Lutao, you don't seem to understand me. This man shows no mercy and has no mercy when it comes to killing. All the victims he was ordered to kill, was with no hesitation, except for one. And if you are right, that task was taken care of. But if you are wrong, he will have no mercy for either of us." The Emperor then went back to his meditating position and said: "To be safe, you better add some more guards around the palace, until we are sure that Yoshima is dead." Lutao breathe in heavy and said: "But my lord, the battle with the Zamuyatsu clan." Emperor calmly replies: "Send in your second in command to lead the army, as for you, you must finish this." Lutao bows and said: "Yes my lord" as he turns and walks back through the corridor into the palace.

LUTAO STANDING WITH HANDS CROSSED

Scene 3
The Desert Walk

The sun is beaming, as the day is getting hotter. The sky is clear and there are no clouds to be seen to add shade. The sun is pounding on the dry desert earth. From the horizon, one can see the vapors rising from beneath the earth surface. From the distance an image slowly appears, the sounds of slow clacker as you see a close up of the horse's hooves slowly taking steps, knowing where the sound is coming from. The horse is breathing heavily as you see an overview of Gori, sitting on the horse as the vultures flew overhead. Then at the side of Gori head, as he is hunched forward with his eyes closed, his hair lies forward as it covers his face. All you can see is a dark image of his eyes. Then the view of Gori's back as it sway from side to side with every step the horse takes as they walk through the steaming desert into the hands of death.

Suddenly the clacking stops. Tired and emotionally exhausted, Gori slowly opens his eyes. They are red and dry; he looks likes he hasn't slept in days. His face and lips are cracked from the desert sun. He closes his eye as if he had nothing left. Moments later he hears a sound, a sound like someone drinking. He slowly opens his eyes again. He looks to the side, to see the horse drinking water. In disbelief they had walked through the desert of the Tochi No Shi (Dry Land of Death) as they called it. Crossing this desert land takes about three days and without any food or water they were sure to die. Legends say that no one makes it out alive. But they did, so it seems. Out of this hell on earth they stumbled on what appears to be a small island, smack in the middle of nowhere. At first he thought it was a mirage as he feels the breeze coming from the pond that is surrounded by trees. It is paradise. Gori then pulls the horses strap to the nearest tree he see's with shade and falls to the ground. He look's up at the horse as the horse slowly fades to black.

GORI ON HORSE (FRONT VIEW)

GORI ON HORSE (SIDE VIEW)

Scene 4
Joining the Imperial Army

Thirteen years ago, at the age of nineteen Gori joined the emperor's imperial army. He worked his way through the ranks without fear. He made the ranks of Shogun by the age of twenty five. But when he was only thirteen, he was good friends with a young prince "Shimatsu Li Tenchu" who is a year older. Tenchu was a lonely child and soon to be emperor, due to his father illness. Tenchu was raised behind the palace walls, where there are rules and the way of life is very discipline. Everything had to be done with perfection. As for Gori, he was raised on the opposite side of the palace walls, where the laws of living are different. Gori was raised by his beautiful mother Shinyin, his father Lingho, also a master and the sword smith and his loving grandmother. Gori also an only child and was taught to respect, have honor and show loyalty for others. Even thou they are both from two different side of the palace wall, they are both learning the art of war. Tenchu is learning his skills from the emperor's top soldier, the shogun and is shown how to live and die by the code of the samurai. Gori

is learning his skills from his parents.
His father shows him how to live and honor
the code of the samurai, that was pass down
from his father. His mother teaches him how
to be graceful in the time of need. And his
grandmother show's him the code of everyday
life. They both learned the code of war
that is how and why they both became good
friends, they understand each other. They
were so close, that they called each other
brothers, and every one in village thought
they were. But they were young, and at times
both stubborn, too young to understand or
to even care about the every day life.

The Yoshima's are a poor family, but
always knew how to manage. Loving life and
enjoying the Earth's freedom. As for Tenchu,
he is always being guarded and feels like a
prisoner in his own home. Tenchu wants what
Gori has, which is the freedom and love he
receives from his parents. That is why he
is always sneaking away from the palace,
to feel free. So he thought his mother the
empress always watched him as he ran off.
She feels proud to let her son run off and
explore the out side world. She knows that
her son is growing up and soon he will be
on his own, running the Imperial Palace.
But she never knew what he was doing when
he was outside of the palace walls. Tenchu
would be hanging around with Gori and a few
of the other guys. And at times they would
steal, mainly from the fruit cart at the
village market. There were times when Gori
and the guys would forget that Tenchu was a

prince, because he fit right in. But on one evening, one of their parents found out what they were doing, and that was the turning point for one of these young men. One day as they were all hanging around, enjoying the fruits of their labor, a seven year old girl approaches them pointing her finger as she stands in front of them and with anger she said: "Gori, you keep this up, you and your friends are going to get caught and all of you will go to prison!"

Gori gives her a strange look and said: "Hay little girl, go away and stop bothering us." The girl look's at him and replies: "If the emperor guard catches you, you…

Gori interrupts her: "We are not worried about the emperor's guards" as he turns at Tenchu and winks. Tenchu jumps in and said: "Yeah, we don't care about those guards, they are all old and ugly too." They all began to laugh. She got so angry that she turns away and said: "Oh you'll see, you won't get away with this any longer!" Then she runs off.

Gori continues to laugh as he looks at Tenchu and said: "Don't pay her any mind she's just a crazy little girl." Tenchu replies: "But she's cute." Gori with a disgust look on his face answers: "Really' what are you crazy too?!" Tenchu blushed and said: "I was just joking," As they all walk off laughing. The day passes as evening approaches; everyone went home except for Gori and Tenchu. He always walks with Tenchu and stands as a look out; and help's him sneak back into the palace. Everything seems fine for the young prince as he past the guards and enters the palace. But thing didn't go as well for Gori when he arrived home. He passes his grandmother as she is sitting on her chair out side the home, laughing at Gori as he walks by. His mother looks at him as she is walking out of the house and calmly said to him: "My son, your father needs to speak with you" and walks off. Gori walks in as the sound of laughter still echoes behind him, and his father on his knees as he is working on a sword. He calls Gori over and calmly asks him: "My son; out of your entire lesson that I have taught you, what is the most important lessons of them all?" Gori nervously ask: Why father? Lingho calmly still working on the sword replies: "Answer me." Gori breaths in and out and answers: "Do not take what is not given."

Lingho puts the sword down and turns to Gori: "Yes my son that is right. Do not take what is not given. Now give it to me." Gori looks at his father and ask: "Give you what?" Lingho stares at Gori and said: "Your hands" Gori looks at his hands as his father continues: "Put your hands out and palms open." Gori eyes widen and he slowly begins to raise his arms. His father pulls out a small bamboo whip, and gives Gori seven lashes on each of palms as he recites the words two more times.

Lingho not proud for what he's done, puts his arm around his son shoulders and tell him: "I love you my son. And I'm sorry we don't have much, but this is not the way to get what you need. Have honor for your self and your families' name. Show honor and respect to everyone that surrounds you and things will appear. Understand?"

Staring at his wounds, tears fell from his eyes as he replies: "Yes father." Gori's mother slowly walks in with a pale filled with cool water. She looks at Gori and said: "Never forget those words and never forget your lesson my son." She turns and looks at her husband as he grabs the pale and helps her put it down as she continues: "Put your hands in the cold water and let it heal for a while, then go to sleep. We'll see you in the morning." She kisses him on top of his head and said: "Sleep on these words, tomorrow begins a new day. Good night son." From that moment Gori finally understood the meaning of honor and respect and said to his parents: "Good night mother, father. I promise I will always honor our family name."

The next day Gori and the guys were just sitting around, just waiting for time to pass. Tenchu then said: "I'm hungry let's go steal some fruits." Every one is willing and Gori first reaction was to do so. But as he uses his hands to get up, the pain in his hands returns. He looks at his palms and the words of his father came to mind. Tenchu know test Gori reaction as he stops and asks him: "What's wrong, Are you okay? You're not turning chicken on us now. Are you?"

Gori shook it off and replies as he is walking towards the fruit cart: "I'm okay; I'll feel even better when I regain my honor." Every one is puzzled as they said to each other: "What??" Gori walks up to the owner and tells him everything. How they were all stealing his fruits when he wasn't looking. At first the owner got upset, and then he tells Gori: "I am mainly upset at myself; I always wondered why I'm always coming up short in my counts everyday." Then he tells Gori: "I always thought I was in a good spot, but I guess I was wrong." Gori puts his head down and tells him: "To earn your respect and regain my honor, I will offer myself to work for nothing, to pay for the fruits my friends and I had taken. We will stand guard and protect your fruits cart from others who tries to steal."

Tenchu and the guys looked at Gori and said: "WE! WHAT DO YOU MEAN WE? We are not in search for any thing." And ran off, still taking the fruits they had in their hands. Gori looks at them as they ran off, then he turns to the owner and said: "I will even work off those." The owner smiles and said: "Okay my name is Kowku" Gori smiles back and said: "My name is Yoshima Gori" he then turns to begin working, guarding the cart.

Six years later, Gori is still standing at the fruit cart. But now he is working along side the owner. Kowku really likes Gori, and he taught him everything he knew about his business, from planting, gardening and how to keep fresh fruits and vegetables. Gori also loves working and learning from Kowku, he has great knowledge about the earth. From time to time Gori still catches a few kids from stealing, but Gori knows what is like not to eat so he would let them go. Sometimes he would let different kids help guard the cart on different days and would pay them by giving them and there family fruits and vegetables. Throughout the years as Gori is working, he is becoming more mature. Standing in the middle of town he sees everything, he watched as all of his friends got in and out of trouble, and realized to him self, if it wasn't for the little girl, he would have been there too. Even though we are still good friends, Tenchu hasn't be coming around as much, ever since I started working and his father became even more ill, things had changed. Gori feels Tenchu is turning cold and heartless.

GORI AS THE YOUNG SHOGUN

Scene 5
The Day of Sorrow

At the age of 21, Tenchu became the youngest emperor. One day he went riding through the village with a few of his guards. There were he saw Nijei, as she is standing their, watching the fruit owner and his helper sell there fruits and vegetables to the public. The emperor stares at her, he was always in love with Nijei he wants her to be his wife one day. Nijei not realizing that the Emperor quietly approached her and stood by her side as she is watching Gori at work and said: "Good evening Nijei." She looks as she was startled: "Oh, you frighten me. Good evening to you, your highness." He looks to her and said: "Tenchu."

Confused she replies: "Excuse me your highness." He smiles and said "Tenchu, you can call me Tenchu. You know Nijei; we've known each other for many years now. I can't have my friends call me highness, but emperor, maybe. He turns away and begins to laugh. She giggles and said "Tenchu, you were always funny." Tenchu turn to her with a smile and said: "Nijei I've been waiting for the right moment to ask you something. She replies: "Yes you're hi, she stops and redirects herself, I mean Tenchu. He looks at her and asked: "Would you like to visit my garden?"

She begins to answer: "Tenchu." Then she pauses for a moment and said: "Thank you, but I can't." Tenchu ask: "Why not my lady? Beautiful flowers must see what real beauty looks like." She giggles and replies: "Thank you once again, but I'm sorry, my family will be waiting for me." The emperor is getting frustrated as he looks away, then calmly said: "Family is important, but nothing will happen to you. You will be safe with me, I promise." Nijei tries to explain: "But I can't…" The emperor interrupts her with anger in his voice: "Why! I can give you anything your hearts desire." Nervously she looks at him and said: "There is someone I'm waiting for." Now Tenchu really gets upset and ask: "Who is he? Tell me who?! And if he loves you, where is he?"

Nijei turns away and bows her head in shame. Tenchu notice and responds in a sarcastic way: "Oh… so that someone you love doesn't love you." Nijei looks at the emperor nervously and said: "Maybe not at this moment, but I know one day we will be together." Then with a sarcastic look on his face, he approaches Nijei and asks her: "So tell me Nijei, who is this person that may never love you?" At first she hesitates. So Tenchu asks the question again and demands an answer "Who, Who is he?" Nijei got upset and blurted out: "It's Gori!"

The young emperor eyes widen with surprise and said to her: "Gori! But he is nothing, he has nothing, look at him, he sells fruits. He has nothing to give you, not even his love. Look at him, he doesn't even see you standing here, he doesn't even know you exist. But for me, I have it all, and I can give you the world." Nijei looks at the emperor and said to him: "Maybe not today, maybe not tomorrow, but I know deep in my heart that one day we will be together." Then she silently turns away and kept watching Gori as he is playing with the kids around him. Tenchu with a deep hate and jealously said to himself: "Gori, what is it about you that everyone loves? Soon we shall see." He gets back on his horse and rides off with his guards, back to palace.

KIDS TAKING FRUITS FROM CART

Scene 6
The Ploy

When Tenchu arrived to the palace, the raw hate and jealously towards Gori continues to consume him. He quickly summons together a small group of soldiers from his new army, and uses them to begin his ploy. He thinks by killing Gori's family, he can take over Gori at his weakest moment, and try to gain the love of Nijei. The young emperor gave out his first order, to the one who is now his first commander, Harugawa the old Emperors shogun, and a small group of soldiers to precede his ploy. Within this group of soldiers is a 33 year old warrior name Lutao, armed and ready to kill as they all march off to fulfill the emporia's orders.

Meanwhile, late that evening as the sun was beginning to set; Gori's parents were home fulfilling there daily actively. On the right side of their house is the cooking area, where his lovely mother Shiyin and grandmother are cooking rice and dumpling for tonight's dinner. They are waiting for Gori to arrive home with some fruits and vegetables to add to there meal. His father Lingho is a great sword smith, known through out Japan for his craft, and also a great swordsman that was pass down from his father who was a great warrior from the Chang Ying Dynasty in China. Lingho then passed it on to his wife and son. He showed them self defense, and the art of the sword. On that evening Lingho was in the back of his home, working on his craft, as he waits for his number one student to arrive. Not knowing from that day on he will never see his son again. Moments later without sound, warriors quietly surrounded Lingho's home as they are getting ready for an ambush. The young warrior Lutao is hiding behind a bush with his bow and arrows at hand, waiting for the orders to shoot. Moments later the order was made by Harugawa to shoot Shiyin. Lutao pulls back on his arrow and calmly breathed in as he took aim he hears his heart beat slows down as he releases the arrow from his fingers. The arrow is heading straight for Shiyin, as she bends down to pick up a dumpling that grand mama had dropped. As she stands up, she see's grand mama with an arrow pierced through her neck. Shiyin look's around to see where it had came from, just to hear a voice yell "ATTACK!" Then out of nowhere soldiers began to jump out of hiding and attacked her. She grabs a knife from the table and throws it into the chest of a soldier that was nearing her as he had his weapon raised. Two other soldiers came around from both side of the table, she quickly crossed her arms and picks up two hot pots filled with boiling rice water and dumpling and tossed it on them, and then she hits them over there head with the pots, knocking them unconscious. Meanwhile at the back of the house, Lingho paused and slightly turns his head to listen to the air, feeling there is something wrong, but without hesitation, he turns back and continues to work on a beautiful sword he is making, as a gift for his son. He taps the tip of the blade checking the balance then he wipes the blade with a cloth dipped in wax. He calmly looks at his reflection with each and every wipe and said to himself "I put my heart and soul in to you, please protect him, become one with him until he passes you on from son to son. Now lets see how well you work." He gets up and walks up to a Bamboo branch and raised the sword to feel the weight and the sharpness of the blade. "Shiinng" He moves the blade across the bamboo branch, slicing it in half. He looks at the blade and said to himself, "Good...Very good, just what he needs." He wipes the blade as he moves onto the next branch. A light breeze whispers through as tension fills the air; for there are three warriors, slowly working there way up to Lingho as he gets into an orthodox position and raises the sword. His focuses on the bamboo branch, he watches it as it sways from side to side, waiting for the right moment to strike. The soldier then focuses in on him. They nodded to each other and slowly begin to move in. The warriors feel their plan is working the moment Lingho strikes his sword they will attack. They feel Lingho will be out of position to defend himself. They all got ready as there is calmness in air. Lingho breathe in, aiming the sword at his target. Knowing he's about to strike the soldiers prepared themselves to attack. Knowing he was being watched, quickly Lingho came down with his sword and at that moment the soldiers attacked. Lingho fakes to strike the bamboo branch, as he then pivots on his left foot 180 degrees, simultaneously countering his attackers with an overhead strike to his left, he quickly steps back with an overhead strike to his right, then stepping inward and another overhead strike down the middle. He looks down at the ground; he had killed the three men in one move. Meanwhile at the front of the house, Shiyin looks in shocked to see more soldiers jumping out of hiding; she could not believe how many there are. And in fear, she runs to the back of the house to where her husband is. As she nearing the back of the house, she sees Lingho standing there. His sword facing back as the blood drips from the blade and three soldiers drop to the ground. He looks up to see her as there eyes lock together, speaking to each other in unspoken words. Suddenly her eyes widen, as a blade pierced through her chest from behind lifting her off the ground. He watched as they tossed her body to the side, where she died instantly. His eyes turn red with anger as he bites down hard, grinding his teeth and breathing rapidly he yells "NNNOOO!!!!" As they all attacked him at once. Lingho quickly picks up another sword, as fifteen warriors surrounded him as they attack him from every angle. He blocks with one sword as he strikes with the other. Fifteen warriors came, and fifteen warriors died, as Lingho stood there covered in there blood. More soldiers came out from hiding and attacked him from all directions. Lingho defends himself as he attacks with both swords, the soldiers tried to block and counter his attack, but failed, and down they went dying one, two, and three at a time. Lingho with both swords striking down with right left, right left, then up the middle slicing them upward from the stomach. He then turns 180 degrees and continues cutting off arms and legs; as the battle went on. From a short distance the shogun sat on his horse watching a great battle unfolded right before his very eyes. He turns and gives an order to his soldiers, as eight of them form a circle around Lingho. Lingho, a true warrior himself, asked no questions to why. He just stood in the center, breathing heavily knowing the end is near. He stares at the swords; his hands are covered in blood as he drops one of them, keeping only the one, the one he made for his son. He position's himself, as he step into a wide stance and his sword facing downward to his left side. At that moment the soldiers raised there swords up to shoulder level. The shogun is watching with enjoyment as the intensity increase. Lingho facing downward as his eyes slowly pans from left to right as he's watching the soldier settled into there stance, indicating that they are ready to attack. He tightly grips the handle of his sword he looks down as the blood flows down his arm. He then takes a deep breath and whispers himself "Gori, take care... my son" and with his right hand he swung his sword to the right in a full circle, as the soldiers came in forward with there's, as their blades penetrates into Lingho. The action stops as there is silence in the air. A light cool breeze brushed through once again, for there was no movement. The shogun watches with intensely, then he orders the soldiers in the field to stand down. Lingho, facing away from the shogun as the blood gushes from his body. He then looks at the soldiers around him as their heads drops from their bodies. The Shogun Harugawa is astounded as Lingho slowly turns around to face him. His blood flow out from his mouth as he looks into Harugawa eyes, rapidly breathing as he is drowning in his own blood, he stabs the sole with his sword. He looks over to where his wife is laying as his breathing is getting shorter and shorter. Then... it stops, the image of his wife begins to fade as he falls to his knees, blood sprays from his mouth as his face hits the ground. The shogun stares at Lingho with honor. A man that was never a real soldier, fought like a mighty warrior until his last breath. He stares at him with admiration as Lingho died next to his sword. The shogun grins as he turns his horse to his men and gives the order to burn the house and he rode off.

LINGHO LAST STAND

Scene 7
The Red Sword

On his way home that evening, Gori sees smoke rising from the same direction. He quickly panic and begins to run as fast as he can, when he got near the house, he see's what seems to be a battle field. There were bodies of soldiers everywhere. Near the cooking table he see's his grandmother, dead on her chair with an arrow lunged in her neck. He looks at her and as he goes to touch her, from the corner of his eye he sees his mother lying on the ground. He runs to her as she feels miles away to see her with a sword through her back and her neck slashed opened. Frighten and scared as tears of fear flows from his eyes. He then runs to the back of the house, where he sees his father, lying in a pool of blood holding onto a sword. To Gori it seems like there are hundred dead soldiers around him. He began to cry as he walks up to his father. Staring at his father for a long moment grasping what might had occurred he bends down and takes the sword from his hand, and made a promised: "One day with this sword I will avenge your death, I swear it." The house burns as he drags their bodies, and tossed them into the burning flames. He sat for hours as he watched his home turn into ashes as it burned to the ground. And with nowhere to go, Gori decided to see Tenchu for help.

The young emperor was expecting Gori arrival and welcomes him in. Gori explains to Tenchu what has happen to his family. Immediately Tenchu calls in one of his guards and give him an order, "I want you to search for any one that might be responsible for this and kill them, bring me there heads." The soldier looks at him and said "Yes my lord." He turns to Gori and tells him "We will find them, and you will get your revenge. But for now, you will stay here and join my army." Tenchu smiles and puts his hand on Gori's shoulder and he said "I have a great idea. Now that I'm emperor, you will become my first in command. Gori looks at Tenchu and replies "I don't understand." Tenchu nudged Gori and went on to say "What's not to understand. I will have the best of my soldier's train you and you'll work your way up the ranks, quickly. And you'll be my personal body guard, my own assassin, my Shogun. What can be better; than a good friend, my best friend standing by my side conquering this land?" Gori looks at him and said: "I'll do any thing; all I want is to avenge my parent's death. No matter who it is, they will die. And if this is what it takes, I kill anyone." Tenchu laughs and said: "And you'll shall my friend, and you shall". But for now, you must get some rest.

Tomorrow I'll take you to the yard where you begin your training." Gori bows and says, "Yes my lord."

Tenchu smiles and said: "Good… Good… you learn fast. This my friend will work well." Then he went on to say: "It sounds good, doesn't it, The Emperor and his best friend ruling Japan.

GORI KNEEING DOWN

Scene 8
The Bad News

The next day, the bad news had spread through out the whole town, that Gori and his family was assassinated. Nijei had heard the news as she was on her way to the market, from a stranger as he was passing by. She stop's and in a nerves tone she ask him "Excuse me sir, what happened?" The stranger stops and tells her "The whole Yoshima family was killed." Nijei eyes filled with tears as she continues to ask him, "The boy, what happened to the boy? Has anyone seen him?" The stranger looks at her and said," I'm sorry my child, but they were all killed." Tears fell from her eyes in disbelief as she put her hand over her face and began to cry. The stranger feels sad for her as he ask "little girl, Are you okay?"

With her watery eyes she looks at him and then she runs off. The stranger looked puzzled and said to himself "I hope she's okay". Nijei run's through the village and heads to the market place. She stops to see the owner closing up his cart and put's a sign out reading no fruits today. She runs up to him as the tears fell from her eyes and she asked him "Gori, Where is Gori?" The owner turns to her, he looks into her sad eyes, and replied "He's gone little girl". Not wanting to believe, she asked him "Will he be back soon?" As he turns away to finish locking up his cart and said, "I'm sorry, but he is never coming back. Something bad has happened to him and his family. He then breathed in and sadly said "I'm going to miss him. He was a good kid and a good friend and one of the best workers I ever had, May the Buddha's bless him and his family." Her tears fell like rain as she cry's even more. He turns to her and asks her "Are you that little girl that is always across the road watching us?" She nods and said "Yes" As she covers her crying eyes. In an attempt to make her smile he said, "I know it wasn't me you were looking at I'm an old, old man." Then he smiles at her, but his smile fades away as her tears fell. He then asks her "You were watching him. So you really liked him yes?" Once again Nijei sadly nods her head. He put's his hand on her shoulder as he kneels down and said with a smile as he attempts to make her smile "To bad I'm too old, It would be nice to be looked at from a beautiful girl from time to time, I'm just an old fossil. She looks at him as he continues: "I'm sorry. I told him you liked him." She puts her hands down and replies: "It feels like a dream." The owner said: "I wish it was but it's more like a nightmare… I'm truly am sorry. I wish he was here. You know, it's getting late; you should go home and say a prayer for him. Maybe you'll see him in your dreams." She looks at him and said: "Thank you, you made me feel a little better." Then he looks at her with a smile and said: "Okay, I hope I still see you around." He gets up and turns around to finish locking up. As she turns to walk home, she bumps into Tenchu. She looks at him with her teary eyes and hugs him tight. She asks him: "Did you hear what happened to Gori and his family?"

Tenchu answers her as he stares over her: "Yes I have. That's why I'm here, to see if you are okay." Then she ask "Who could have done this to them?" He replies as he holds her: "I don't know, but I know you loved him. And it would be wrong for me to leave you all alone." She pulls away as she replies: "What are you saying Tenchu?" He pauses for a moment then he said: "It would be in his memory, as it would be my deepest honor, for me to take his place in loving you." She looks at him, and he continues to say: "Nijei… I love you, I always in love with you and nothing would make this emperor happier then to be with the woman he loves. Maybe not at this moment, but in time, you will learn to love me the way you love him." She hesitates as she looks at him with a smile and said: "Maybe" as she lets him go and walks off. He then turns away with a grin and says to him self: "My plan is working."

NIJEI (GORI WIFE)

Scene 9
Getting To Know a Friend

It's a beautiful day over the village of OMI and Gori is home with his family. His loving wife as she is cooking the meal of the day, as his baby girl sits by her side. As he is laughing and playing around the house with his boys Tomo and Ushi as they take a pail of water and throws it on him. Suddenly he awakes calling out there names, not knowing he's just been a sleep for the past two days. As he fully awakes and opens his eyes he said: "Oh it's you" The horse looking over him with water dripping from his mouth as to say: "Wake up" Gori then said to himself: "Dame, it was only a dream." Yawning and stretching he slowly get's up and said: "I wish this was a dream." He takes a step forward as he stares out into the waters and squints his eyes into focus as he pans around as he scratches his rear and asks: "Is this a pond or a lake?" The horse just shook his head; Gori looks at him and said: "I don't know either." He continues to pans around, he stops and he stares at the horse, still in disbelief and asked: "Where are we?"

The horse shook his head as to say: "I don't know" Gori then realizes that they had just walked through the desert. He grabs the horse's straps and pets him on the head and tells him: "Thank you for saving me." The horse nods his head to say: "You're welcome" Gori looks at him and said: "You know friend, I don't know your name, and you seem like a smart horse, so I'll call you Ereganto (intelligent). What do you think?" The horse shook his head and breathes out as to say: "No" Gori laughs as they are both walking, looking for a good spot to settle down. Gori replies: ""No why not? I think that's a good name for you". The horse stops and stomps his front hove to insist he doesn't like that name. Gori then said with a laugh: "Okay, Okay... Well since you are also a stubborn horse, I will call you Pinattsu (Peanut). The horse nods his head as to say: "Yes" Gori looks at the horse with a twitch in his eye and said: "So you like that one?" The horse nods his head again as he made a happy sound, that he likes that name. Gori then replies: "I don't like it, but if you do, so be it. You're the one that has to live with it," then he laughs. Pinattsu then nudged Gori with his head. "Hay I was only joking" He stops and pets the horse on the head and said: "This looks like a good spot to settle down, underneath the trees and near the lake, I think this will do, what do you think Pinattsu?" Pinattsu nods his head to say: "Yes"

Gori looks at Pinattsus' legs, which has cuts and bruises and his hooves were covered with mud and dry blood. Gori himself did not look to well, but he feels Pinattsu needs to be taken care of first. Gori looks into Pinattsu eyes and tells him: "You took care of me, when you walked through this hot desert, and saved my life. Now I'm going to take care of you. And I see we have everything we need here for both of us to get better, so let's get started." Gori pulls off the horse saddle and armor and toss it to the side. He then stares at everything Pinattsu had carried on his back, as they crossed the steaming desert. Gori looks at him with amazement, as he walks him over to the lake. He glanced around and found some plants that will help heal the wounds. Then he took off his blooded keikogi, as the strip of cloth falls out. He looks at it for a moment as it gently floats on top off the blue waters. His mind became a blur as he smells the scent of his wife as he reflected on what happened to them that day. He then picks it up and ties it around head, and begins to wash the blood off the horse. After rinsing Pinattsu off, he tears the sleeves off his keikogi into four strips, he then places the leaves around the wounds and wraps his legs with the strips. Gori then begins to scrape the bottom of Pinattsu's hooves. When he was done, he puts a blanket on his back to dry and keep him warm. He then pulls an apple from a near by tree and gives it to him, as he pets him on the side of his head and said in a calm voice: "Eat up my friend, we must regain our strength." The sun was beginning to set as he stares out into the waters. The shine of the reminding sun glitter off the water as Gori takes off his pants and runs into the lake. He washes the dirt and blood off his body by using the leaves he got for Pinattsu. While in the lake he sees fishes as they swim pass him. Gori takes a deep breath and slowly went under the water, moments later he walks on shore with two fishes he had caught.

Night approaches, Gori begins to dig a small hole in the ground. He then puts some twig with some dry leaves into the hole and lights it on fire by smacking two small stones together. As the flames lights up the darkness, Gori rolls out a sleeping matt from the horses saddle and sit's near the fire. With his tanto knife he slice open one of the fishes he had caught and begins to eat it. As he sits there chewing, he stares into the flames as his mind begins to wonder. Moment later he takes the cloth off from around his head and unravels a tie that is holding his long braided hair together. With his fingers, he combs his hair forward and from mid point he cuts his hair off. Then he pulls his hair back and ties it, using his wife's cloth. He looks at Pinattsu and tells him: "Let's get some rest, tomorrow we begin." He rolls over onto his side and went to sleep. The next morning, Gori is still sound asleep was once again awoken by a splash of water. He opens his eyes as he is gasping for air, and there stands Pinattsu looking down at him nodding his head with a horses laugh as to say: "Its time to get up" Gori ask him as he rubs his eyes: "Is this going to happen every morning?" Pinattsu once again nods his head showing his teeth. "Okay" as Gori rolls up the mat and said: "You're right my friend, its time to get to work". He gets up yawning as he's looking at Pinattsu and said: "We are going to begin this morning by strengthening our bodies". Pinattsu looks at Gori and with a deep breath he walks away. Gori yells: "Hay where you're going? I thought we were in this together?" Pinattsu just kept walking away, and then Gori yells: "Okay!! I will do the training myself and you can just watch!" Pinattsu then stops and turns to him and nods his head.

Before Gori begun his training, he said to Pinattsu: "Dame Lazy horse, that's what I should have named you, Dame lazy horse." Pinattsu laugh as Gori begins his training. He starts by stretching his body as he bends forward and then side to side loosening up his muscles. Then he strengthens his body, with pushup, then pull-ups from a near tree branch, squats to strengthen his legs and sit ups. Days had pass, as he is now beginning to feel stronger. He then begins to work on his inner strength, by slowly breathing in, then out and tensing every part of his body, as he is also developing his mental balance. Days later he feels even stronger, then he begins to work on his fighting technique his father had taught him. Days pass as it became weeks, weeks pass as they became months and every day Gori continues to train harder. Standing in the center of a small forest, surrounded by trees he continues to practice his craft for hours. He only uses one of the swords to practice his Bushido with {the way of the warrior}. He hung up a few coconuts around the forest to work on his striking techniques, by slicing them in half with every move. At night as Gori sat by the fire he would make weapons, like bow and arrows he carved out of a bamboo and tree branches. Using fruits from the trees as targets he practice shooting them on horse back from 100 yards away. He also made some wooden darts out of tree stems. Gori is always working on something, even when he's relaxing; he would be working on something. He even made two bamboo hats for Pinattsu and himself for the long trip back through the hot desert. He also hand knits together two blankets for Pinattsu and himself for those cold nights by using thin vines that hung from the trees. Months pass, and it's been almost a year as the day has finally came for Gori to make the trip back and retrieves his redemption.

For his return trip, he will wear black from the armor he had taken from one of the soldier on that morning, and with a thin vine he ties the lower part of the hakama and the forearm of his keikogi. Then he puts on his white sleeveless jacket (keikogi) and his straw hat. The horse's armor Gori left on the ground, he only puts on Pinattsu a blanket, and the strap that went around his head and a bamboo hat that Gori made him. Gori then picks up his tanto knife and puts it between his hip and belt strap. The other two swords he straps one around the horses neck and his fathers sword, he straps around his back. As he is tying everything down, he looks at Pinattsu and said: "My friend, we must travel the way we came. So we must travel light. We have plenty of water that I put into coconut shells and some fruits that will only last for about two, maybe three days." Pinattsu nodded his head. "We'll travel most of the way by night and we'll rest by day. We'll try to stay cool with this shade I made by braiding vines together." Gori grabs the remaining gear and throws it into the lake. He takes the sword he used to practice with and plunged it into the tree stump he camped under. He then walks over and climbs on his horse, looks up to the heavens and said: "Thank you my lord; for this miracle in the desert. Please bless our journey once again." He pats Pinattsu on the side of his long neck and tells him: "You know we will never find this place again." Gori then pans around for the last time, at the place that was there home for the past nine months. He then asks Pinattsu: "Are you ready? Pinattsu nodes his head. "Okay, let's go." As he slaps the straps and they rode off, vanishing into the steaming horizon.

Scene 10
The Imperial Wedding

Six years ago the old emperor had passed away due to illness, making his son Tenchu one of the youngest emperors in their Dynasty. Within those six years as Tenchu ruled the land his love for Nijei grows strong. Everyday he persuades her to fall in love with him, and with in time she has, but not deeply. Maybe in her heart she feels she needs to be with someone that is deer to her and Tenchu is. Six years pass and it is now their wedding day. Everything is beautiful in the middle of the royal garden, surrounded by his family and his lovely flowers, the gongs rang as the ceremony begins. The emperor is standing there with two of his top guards. While his first in command and his top soldiers are guarding the outside the palace. His first commander is the shogun Gori. Gori now twenty five, is a mighty shogun warrior for the emperor, and only does what told, no questions asked.

Then the sounds of drums, as it vibrate in a one, two rhythm and the Buddha monk's walks out in pairs, chanting a prayer as they bless the ceremony. The emperor proudly stands there with one of his cousins and his two of guards, on the platform waiting for the arrival of his bride. He is wearing a gold and red takishido. Then he sees her, as the monks are escorting her down the path of the gate of supreme harmony as she walks in the center. The bride is wearing a beautiful gold and yellow wanpisu Kimono that drapes on the ground stretching ten feet long. Hundreds of his family members and guests are attending the ceremony, as they are here to witness the young emperor's marriage. She walks her way through the colorful garden and nearing the platform to where the groom awaits. But as she nears, thoughts of Gori begins to enter her mind. She begins to slowly slow down to a halt as the monks continue to walk on. Everyone there thinks its all part of the ceremony. The emperor looks at her and asks in a silent whisper: "My love... Are you alright?" She looks into his eyes, as the tears formed. She gets down on her knees and bows her head. He knows what to come as she said: "I'm sorry my lord... But, I am not ready for this, I love you but I'm not deeply." The emperor eyes widen with anger, not to make a scene he calmly replies: "If you are not ready we'll get married another time, next month or next year, it does not matter when, I'll wait for you. I will wait for the time to be right, because I love you." Her tears fell to the ground as she replies: "I know you do, and I thought I could, but it can never be... my heart still belongs to another. And when he died, so did the feelings for me to love again, has died with him." Tenchu said to himself: "Gori… everything I've done and still she's in love with him. When this is over, I will settle this ones and for all." She stood up and with her watery eyes she looks at him and said: "I'm sorry your highness, please forgive me" and ran off. Tenchu slowly turns to his guards and with his eyes he gives a silent order to retrieve his future wife.

The empress see's him and did not agree as she quickly steps in and yells: "STOP! Disregard those orders." The soldier looked at the emperor as they stopped and stood back at attention. She then turns to him, with sorrow in her eyes and said: "Let her go my son." Tenchu stares at his mother with inner anger and embarrassment as she continues to say: "I know you love her and she tried, she truly tried to love you, but her heart is not with you, it is somewhere else." He turns to the direction she ran and stares as he feel's hurt and empty inside. Then again a heat of inner rage irrupts inside and the look of revenge fills his eyes as he calmly replies to his mother: "Yes mother, you are right. You're always right." The empress turns to the guests and said: "I'm sorry for your troubles, Please forgive what you have just seen you all may leave." The crowd is now confused as they look at one another, they slowly got up and began to leave the palace.

The emperor walks back to his chamber and demands to see Gori too finish this once and for all. Gori not knowing on what had just occurred received the message from one of the guard as he is posted outside the palace walls. He enters the emperor chambers, and kneels down on one knee and said: "My lord, you summoned me." The emperor with his back turn as he is facing the window and said: "Gori, you are the best of all of my assassins. Every order you received, were executed immaculately. You always showed courage and honor. And as my friend, you always showed me respect." Gori bows his head and replied: "Thank you my lord, it's my honor." The emperor turns from the window and looks at Gori and continues to say: "I have a secret mission for you." Gori still on his knee, with his head down replies "Yes my lord." Tenchu continues to say: "I want you to assassinate Tanglu and his family. They live outside of the village gates. Take a few men with you." Gori with no hesitation and emotion answers: "Yes my lord, as you wish." Tenchu stares at him and said: "That's what I mean Gori, I give you an order and with no remorse and with no emotion, it is done. You're a heartless killer." Gori looks up at the emperor and replies: "As your shogun and as a soldier, I will always honor my emperor wishes." Gori turns to the side and continues to say: "But as your friend, the heartless one is the one who gives the orders." He then bows his head down. The emperor turns to the window with his arm crossed behind his back and said: "Gori… do you know that you put fear into everyone." Gori replies: "No my lord, I'm just carrying out my orders." Tenchu continues: "All of who you know and all of whom you don't, fear you. And as a long time friend of mine, I fear you too." Gori looks at the emperor as he went on to say: "I knew I made the right choice, on that evening you came to the palace." Gori got up, and fixed his armor. He bows his head and replies: "Thank you my lord". At that moment the emperor turns and looks out of his window into his garden and said: "No one betrays or dishonors me, no one." He turns to leave the emperor chamber to fulfill his orders and replies: "Yes my lord."

MONKS WALKING DOWN THE PATH

Scene 11
The Assassination of the Tanglu Family

It's nearing midnight, as four night soldiers are approaching the home of Tanglu and his daughter. They were sleeping as Tanglu was awoken, as he heard a noise coming from the outside. He knows it has something to do with his daughter. So he quietly awakened her and tells her "You must hide." Nervously she asked "Why father?" He replies as he rushes her along "The emperor wants you dead and he'll do anything to succeed. So you must hide quickly in this underground shed I built for this very reason." She looks around nervously as she is being shoved downward and said to her father "In here?" nervously he answers "Yes, and you must hurry, there's no time." As she is quickly stepping down into the shed he tells her "No matter what happens or what you hear, stay in here until sun rise. Once its clears, run as far away as you can." Nijei started to cry, Tanglu brushed the tears from her eyes and kisses her on her head and said "I love you, my butterfly… your mother and I will be watching down on you from the heavens." Then he slowly closes the hatch as she looks up at him with her teary eyes. Tanglu shuts the hatch and covers it with an old chair. He turns and grabs his sword; he kicks the door that leads to the front yard wide open, just to see a dark image standing ten feet in front of him. Tanglu jumps back in fear as the warrior stood looking undeviatingly at him. Tanglu frighten but grips his sword, knowing he has to protect his only daughter from the emperor killers. He raises his sword up to shoulder level, as his eyes widen with anger as he yells "AAAAA!!!!" and runs charging straight forward at the dark warrior. Then suddenly out of no where "SHOUHT", "SHOUHT", "SHOUHT" As Tanglu arches his back, as he was strucked by three arrows from different directions, dropping him face first into the ground. The dark shadow slowly walks up to Tanglu, as he lays there dying in a pool of his own blood, and barely breathing, fighting to stay alive. The dark warrior then takes off his helmet as he shoves Tanglu body onto his back. He pulls out his sword to finish his suffering, as he gives orders the other soldiers "Check the house and kill anyone inside, then set it on fire." The soldier replies "Yes sir" as they went onto fulfill his orders. Tanglu barely alive, slowly open's his eyes and looks into the eyes of the shogun as he is raising his sword. Then, with a dying breath Tanglu whispers "It is you." The shogun take's a step back. Tanglu barely breathing as the blood poured from his mouth "Ssshheee, al-waysss thought- yo-you were dead". The Shogun looks down at him and with anger he steps on the man's chest and ask "Who is she, dying man?" Tanglu holds on to the shogun foot as his chest is being crushed and trying to breath as he gasping for air, and said "M…y… daug…hter Nijei." The Shogun steps off him and replies "Nijei? You mean, the little girl from across the road?" Tanglu answers as he look up at Gori "Yes… and you are here… to kill her." The shogun looks down at him and said "Those are my orders, to kill you and your family. All these years, I did not know she was still alive and that you were her father." And with the last of his breath Tanglu said, "She didn't… marry… the emperor, because, she is still… ii…n love with you……" she is my life… Please- please take care of her." Then his eyes closed as his soul left his body.

The shogun turns to his soldier as they started to burn the house. He asked them "have you found anyone?" The soldier responds "No sir, there was no one inside." At that moment in side of the house, Nijei climbs out from hiding place and quickly grab her father short sword (Wazachi). Then she slowly crawls to the window and tries to look outside from the lower corner of the window edge. But the smoke is so thick it made it hard for her to see anything. But as the smoke slowly moves through the air, she sees her father, lying on the ground. She inhales as she gasps for air and begins to cry in silent. The soldiers are standing over him, as she sees one of them with his helmet off, giving orders to one of them, the soldier bowed and then quickly left. She try's to look through the smoke as it is getting thicker. Suddenly she see's a familiar image and quickly turns away. Her heart begins to beat faster, as if she has just seen a ghost. She thought to herself "No… It can't be." She turns back and try's to take another look, but the smoke is getting thicker as it is filling the air, and it's begins to fill the inside of the house, making it harder for her to breathe. She begins to cough in silence, holding in what she can, trying hard to pierce through the black thickening smoke. And just then, for a single moment, the smoke vanished, leaving a clear view for her to see. And standing ten feet away from her is the one she always loved, ever since she was a little girl. But now, the boy she once loved is standing over the man she loved all her life...her father. She turns away, as thoughts and images runs through her mind, of the events that had occurred in her life, from her past up to the present moment. Her demeanor had increasingly changed from sadness to anger, and without hesitation she runs out of the burning house yelling his name. G O R I!!!

He looks up at her, as she is charging at him with a short sword. It was only a few yards, before was she caught with an arrow on the side of her arm, forcing her to the ground. She laid there screaming in pain, calling out his name "G O R I!! WHY!!" The soldiers begin to approach her to finish her off, as Gori yells: "STOP!" He walks' up to her, and intensely looks down at her and said: "You must desire death." She looks into his eyes, screeching in pain as the blood flows from her arm and said: "Y… you must… have no desire… for life" and fell unconscious. At that moment Gori felt something inside; something he hasn't felt, since he was a little boy. The words of his father came to mind "Do not take what is not given". One of the soldiers looks at Gori and said: "We must finish her." Gori looks at him as the soldier raises his sword and continues to say: "Our orders are simple, to kill them all." Gori steps in the way and said: "NO!!" As he is looking down at her. The soldier replies: "But those are the wishes of the emperor." Gori slightly turns his head to the left and looks at him then he slowly turns to the right, to look at the other soldier and said: "I'm here, not the emperor and these are my orders." The soldier to his left replied: "You're disobeying and dishonoring the emperor orders." The soldier to his right takes a step back and raises his sword in an attack position and said: "This is treason!" Gori stood there with his sword in hand, the point of the blade is facing the ground as he replies: "NO, this is not treason, this is life. A life we shall not take." Suddenly the soldier to his right lunges his sword, aiming straight for Gori chest. Within a split second, Gori shift his shoulder as he brings his blade upward, catching the enemies blade, between his own blade and armor. Gori looks at him and said "You have just made the wrong move." The other two soldier were surprised, as he begin to withdraw his swords from there scabel. But before he could even begin to pull it out, Gori counters with a low sideway motion as he slice open the belly of the soldier to his right who attacked first then coming over with his blade, slicing his neck wild open with an inward motion. Then within one motion, Gori steps into an angle swinging the blade over and around his head, bringing it downward to his left, cutting off the head of the soldier to his left, still with the soldiers sword in his scabel. The third soldier, sitting on his horse had seen the whole event take place as begins to ride off to the south. Gori quickly picks up another sword and throws it. As the soldier gallops' a whistle comes from behind as the swords cuts through the dark air. "SWELL" "SWELL" "SWELL" "SHUNK!" as the steal of blade pierce through the armor and the back of the soldier as he continues to ride off to warn the emperor. Gori recognizes he doesn't have much time, walks over to see Nijei as she is lying in her own blood. Still unconscious Gori knows this is the only time he has to help cure her. Once the emperor gets word, that Gori had committed treason on him, he will send more soldiers out to find and kill him. First he immediately takes a blade and lowers it into the burning fire, then he grabs both sides off the arrow and brake off the point then quickly pulls it out. He takes the blade from the fire then and places the flat surface of the blade on to her wound. He holds her tight as he lowers the blade on to her skin. The smell of burned skin fume the air as she suddenly begins to kick and scream then fell unconscious again. Then he takes some leaves from a near by bush and chews on it, then spreads it on to her wounds, he tears a strip of cloth from her gown and wraps it around her arm. He picks her up, and puts her onto his horse. She sits hunch over as he got on, he holds her as they rode off, vanished into the darkness. Meanwhile, the wounded soldier made it to the palace gates, where there are two guards on watch. The horse stops as the soldier fell off. The guards looked at each other, and then rush to the man aid. And in his dying words he tells them what had occurred. The guards ask him "Who's done this to you?" He barely could say the name, but he mentions "Gori" before he died. The head guard tells the other: "Go and informs the emperor." The guard rushes to the emperor chamber, walks in, gets down on one knee and said: "Excuse me your highness we just received some information from one of the soldiers that was out on one of your mission." The emperor staring out his window with his arms crossed behind his back replies: "Go on." The guard looks up at the emperor and said "My lord its Gori, he has dishonored you by committing treason." The emperor turns to the guard and said: "He what? No one betrays me, no one!" Get me Lutao!" And he turns back to the window. The guard replies as he bows his head: "Yes my lord" and went off. Tenchu then thinks to himself: "I thought this plan would work… what happen?"

Moments later, Lutao walks into the emperor chambers with one of his guards, his younger brother (Takamuri). They both got down on one knee as Lutao said: "My lord, you summoned me?" The emperor turns away from viewing his garden and said: "Yes, I'm promoting you; you are now the shogun and the leading commander of the imperial army". Lutao is surprised as he looks at Takamuri, then looks at the emperor and said: "Thank you my lord, I will honor you." The Emperor sat on his thrown and said: "Good, now for your first mission, I want you to find Gori and the girl and kill them both." Lutao looks at the emperor and replies: "My lords are you sure?" The emperor gets up off his throne and came down to Lutao's level, he grabs Lutao by his chin and stares at both sides of his face, he then looks deep in to his eyes and said: "Make sure this will be the last time you ever question my authority. The next time I'll have your head." Tenchu looks into his eyes and said: "You will do, but you'll never be like him." Tenchu pushes Lutao's face away, as he stood up, he then said: "My orders are very simple, find them both and kill them! No matter what it takes, kill them both! Now Go!! Lutao and his brother both bowed there heads and said: "Yes my lord" As they get up and walk out of the emperor's chamber.

Tenchu then said to himself as he sat back on his throne: "Now the search begins."

TANGLU BATTLE

Scene 12
The Emperor Last words

Late that evening Gori wears a black uniform and a dark mask to cover his face. He looks up and begins to scale the eastern wall of the emperor palace. Once inside, he quickly and quietly work's his way through the halls and down the step as he is looking for the emperor, and the emperor's men patrolling the palace floors, so he does what has to be done to get to Tenchu. Gori a dark assassin killing off all of the emporia's military personnel. He would quietly grab them from behind and pull there head back and slices there throats open. With others he would come from behind and cover there mouth and stabs them in the chest or strangle them with a thin wire. He is working his way to the emperor's garden knowing that's where he'll be, he sees two soldiers guarding the entrance of the corridor forbidding anyone to enter. Gori slowly pulls out a wooden straw from a pouch he has around his waist and four wooden darts dipped in poison. He takes one of the darts and puts it into the straw, he slowly aims at the guard that is closest to him then blew, hitting him on the side of the neck. As the other soldier turns to see what has transpired, he also got hit on the side of neck. They both fell and died instantly.

Gori quietly steps out of the darkness as he pans around the area to see if any one is coming, then quickly walks through the corridor. As Gori passes through he sees the emperor sitting in the middle of his garden with his back turned. He pulls off his mask as he begins to step quietly to his direction. The emperor knows that Gori is coming from behind. So he slightly turns his head, looking back from the corner of his eye and said: "I knew you be coming for me... You were certainly the best of the best". The emperor turns his eyes forward and continues: "but are you really the best. For all these years I've known you, I would have never thought you would betray me."

Gori stares at him as he standing behind him replies: "The night my parents were killed, I had no where to go and no one I can turn to, so I came to you, and when I did, at the time I felt heartless, I was angry, I had hate for everyone. You were my only friend, the only one I knew that could help me. But you used me, like you use everyone that surrounds you. And on that morning, when your men arrived at my home and killed my family, those same feelings of hate and anger had once again returned. And even more so, because this time, I knew it was you." Tenchu breathe in and replied: "Hatred... you are and will always be an assassin, nothing but a heartless Killer".

Gori begins to step closer as he answers: "An assassin a killer, yes. But heartless never, the only heartless man here is you. It's always been you, even when we were young; for some reason you grew up to envy me. Why?" Tenchu laughs with an angry voice and said: "Why? Why you ask… You out of all had nothing, but still had everything. A family that loved you, they always treated you with respect. Not like I, the royal family treated me like I was some kind of pet. On that evening when you came to me, yes I took you in. And as your emperor I decided to make you the first in command, the shogun of the imperial army, the only one who can rule this part of Japan, next to me." Tenchu closes he eyes and with anger and continues to say: "Gori, I trusted you! And out of all that I in trust, you… you betrayed me and dishonored the imperial palace! And to me as your friend, you took the only one I have ever loved!" Gori steps closer and answers: "No Tenchu. We stopped being friends the night you gave me order to kill her." Tenchu smirks as he replies: "You know Gori it took seven long years; and I still managed to fulfill my orders, and more." Gori digs his foot into the ground as he moves in closer and said: "That's why you are going to die."

Tenchu arches his back as he calmly inhales then exhales as he said: "Gori… Think for a moment. Do you really think that is when? Do you think it was a coincidence on that evening that you showed up?" For a moment Gori stops as he questions: "What do you mean, it was you?" Tenchu pauses as for there was silence, he then answers "Yes Gori… it was I. Me. I planned the whole thing. Even when we were young, I knew she loved you and I hated you for that. That was the moment that I ended our friendship. The funny thing is, at the time you never knew. You never knew she loved you, But I did. That is why on that same evening, I order the assassination of your parents and that you would come to me." Gori stares at Tenchu as Tenchu continues: "You see Gori, it goes back even further. The funny thing is, you had no idea"

Memories' of his family flashed in his mind as tears of anger fills his eyes. He tightly grips the handle of his sword and said: "You took everything I ever loved in this world from me, my parents, my children, and my wife." Gori breathes in and slowly steps closer as he is pulling out his sword and he asks: "Why did you do this to me? I thought we were brothers."

Tenchu answers without a care: "You see Gori, for me, even with all this, I had nothing, and deep inside I felt empty. I wanted you to feel the way I felt all my life, I wanted you with nothing." Gori stares at the Emperor and steps even closer as he raises his sword. Tenchu looks back from the corner of his eyes and continued to say: "I know that my end is near, so I will tell you this." Gori with his sword raise as he replies: "There is nothing you can say that will save you." Tenchu chuckles and said: "That's what I always loved about you Gori, SHOW NO MERCY. But if I am right about you, which I know I am, you'll be searching for the one who killed your wife, the one who used the sword that took her life." Gori as he positions himself into a perfect angle answers: "Yes I will."

Tenchu went on to say: "So I will tell you this, Lutao ran off into the mountains. He is living somewhere high up the Takai Yama Path." Gori still in position ask: "So why tell me this, now that your end is near?" Tenchu looks up at the blue sky as the clouds slowly moves over head and replies: "I don't know, maybe because you are a friend… Or maybe, to save my soul before I die." Gori answers: "We are not friends and you don't have a soul, So Why?" Tenchu laughs as he replies back to Gori: "Like I said many times, No one, I mean no one, betrays me. Lutao is nothing but a coward; he should have been here with me right by my side like a true warrior. So you see Yoshima, even in the moment of death, I will still find a way to save face." Tenchu arch his back as he breaths in smelling his flowers for the last time. Gori looks at the emperor with disgrace and said: "You are a man with no loyalty and no honor. You take life for granted and you took what was not given. You took every thing from me and turned me into what I once was, your Shogun, your commander your killer." As Gori speaks, the energy to kill the Emperor flows through his body and into his hands as he continues to say: "I never dishonored you. No matter what orders you gave me, they were all carried out with honor, the honor in which you no longer have and the love that you will never receive. My parents gave me life and my wife turned me into what I am. But for you." "SWISH, SHING" At that moment Gori swung his sword downward as the blade across Tenchu's neck and the blood sprayed onto his flowers. Gori stares at Tenchu's lifeless body as it twitch it last nerve and said: "DEATH IS WHAT YOU DESERVE!"

As Tenchu body and head fell to the ground, the Empress watches from a faraway window, she said to herself "My son... you made your own destiny." Then she turns away. Gori kneels and wipes the blood off his blade on the emperor clothing and said: "This is for my family." Puts the blade back into its case and heads off in search of LUTAO.

TENCHU STANDING WITH SWORD

Scene 13
IN SEARCH FOR LUTAO

Days pass, since Gori rode off in search for Lutao. Nearing the mountain he sees a path that leads upward. And a small sign that read "The Takai Yama Path" (The Highest Mountain). Gori pats the horse on the head and said: "We are near my friend. Now it is time to seek our revenge and end this once and for all." He holds the horses strap as they head up the path. The higher they went it began to get colder and the trees covered with snow. Midway up the mountain, Gori stops and gets off his horse. He pulls out his sword from the side of the horse's saddle, and tells Pinattsu: "I'm sorry my friend, this is where it ends for you. From here on, it's between me and him." The horse shook his head as to say: "No!" Gori pats Pinattsu on his side and said: "It's not your battle, and for him to take another life from me, I don't know what I'll do, I think I'll go mad." Gori walks to the front of the horse and tells him: "I know you're stubborn, but this time you must listen to me. Go back down the mountain and wait for me. If I'm not down by sunset, go, understand… I know you understand." He pats the horse on the side of his head and said: "Thank you. You are a true friend." Then Gori goes on his way, as Pinattsu just stood there. Pinattsu turns his head around and looks back at Gori, Gori turns around and looks back to see Pinattsu, maybe for the last time. He raise his hand and wave goodbye, the horse nodes his head then heads down the path. Gori turns to continue his journey up the mountain. On his way up, he mentally prepares himself for war, saying to himself as he is looking up: "Today is the day of death and Lutao… now it's your time to die."

As he nears the top, he sees a small house covered with light snow. And from the distance he sees Lutao standing outside with his arm crossed, as he is waiting for the moment of Gori's arrival. The sky is turning gray as dark cloud begins to hover over them. There eyes lock, as it begins to rain, slowly washing away the snow. Gori raises his left arm and points at Lutao as he said: "My search for you is now over, and so is your life." Lutao with his arm still crossed, as his fingers are touching the handle of his sword, replies: "Now that you found what you're looking for, come take it." Lightning struck down from the dark sky as they stare at each other, preparing for battle.

Scene 14
The Battle of Two Warriors

Somewhere up in the cascade, near the mountain peaks, known as the place of harmony. Gori and Lutao finally meet for there final battle. The sounds of thunder rumbles thought the air as Lutao pulls out his sword and points it at Gori from across the covered deck and said: "The Emperor once told me, you were a great warrior, even greater then I." Gori looks pass his words and reflect to the day he killed his wife. Lutao steps forward and said, "Now we shall see who is greater." Taking off the white cloth, Gori unleashes his hair and ties it around the handle of his sword. Then he slowly pulls the blade out from his case and said: "This cloth resembles the sole of my wife, and today she will see you die." The rain falls from the sky, hitting the leaves from the trees and the soil on the ground, as the water from the heavens, makes the earth soft. For a moment there is silence, there eyes still locked together, as the rain drips from their faces. Gori tells Lutao: "Now its time to face your end, along side your Emperor." Then the sound of two blades shifts though the air, as both warriors get into there fighting stance. Tension arose as cold sweat runs down their faces. Gori takes a deep breath... and the same for Lutao. No room for fear for these two warriors, as they get ready for battle. There's only one thing in there minds, to kill or be killed. But for one, to retrieve the revenge he's been longing for, and too avenge his families' death. They both push off, the sound of running foot steps as they run across the muddy yard. Lutao from the east and Gori from the west, both with their swords raised as they are coming to each other with an overhead strike. "CHING" as there swords met. Their eyes engaged as they are inches from each other. It was only seconds that had pass, which felt like minutes, but in their minds, it felt like an eternity, as they both tried to use there strength against one another, but neither one gave way. Then simultaneously they both pulled back grasping for air, both true warrior as they stare at each other, for the moment, they are both equal. Lutao gives Gori an evil grin and said: "This is either going to be a long night or a short evening."

They both took a step back and stared at each other. Gori replies: "No matter which, but by the end you will be dead." Once again the sound of swords as it cuts through the air. "Ching, Ching" as there blades met with a double over head strike. Lutao quickly moves inward striking Gori with a leading elbow to the face and within the same momentum, Lutao spins around striking Gori to the midsection with a spinning back kick, pushing him back a few steps. Gori holds his stomach with his left hand, as he looks at Lutao, and sees a smirk forming on his face. Gori swiftly gets into a wide stance, bracing his sword up to shoulder level. Then he attacks, striking with a downward motion to the right then left, then aiming low, to cut off Lutao's legs. Lutao quickly steps back and blocks both attacks, Gori then rams his head into his face. Lutao falls back as the blood runs down his nose. With no expression Gori looks at Lutao, Lutao stares back as the rains falls washing away the blood from their faces. Lutao's eyes slightly widen in fear, and to Gori that a sign of weakness. Then it began the battle to the end between two warriors. Back and forth they went, as there swords slice through the thin air, "Ching, Ching" as the steal from their swords clashed. The battle went on and on. Gori then leaps into the air swinging his sword outward with his right hand. The tip of the blade slightly misses Lutao as he pulls back and turns his head to the left and watches as the blade pass, to see his own reflection. Lutao spun around a few times as he was moving backwards and fell to the ground. Gori point his sword at him and said: "As much as I want this to be over, I'm not going to kill you the way you killed my family." Gori steps back as he gives space for Lutao to get up and continues to say: "I'm going to watch you die as I kill you where you stand." Lutao said to himself as he slowly gets up: "I must be prepared, this might be a trick" he gets up without harm and said as they both get ready: "Yoshima by giving me this chance, it may cost you your life." Gori replies: "We shall see." Then the battle continued. They begin fighting there way down the Takai Yama Mountain. For the moment Gori has the upper hand, as he is fighting from the higher level of the path, striking down hard with every step he takes. Lutao takes advantage, as Gori charged with an over head strike from his left, striking downward to the right side of Lutao's head. Lutao in an orthodox position squats into a low stance, blocking Gori's attack with an upward block. He then steps inward, as they ride there blades together hearing the sound of steal approaching nearing the tusba, Lutao flips the blade and slice Gori on his upper arm. Lutao continues to spin around, striking Gori to the face with a spinning back elbow strike. Knocking him to the ground, as Gori drops his sword. Lutao then came charging at Gori to end this war once and for all, plunging his sword straight down the middle to Gori's chest. Gori on the ground, position himself, laying flat on his back, as he times Lutao's actions as he is coming down with full force, and catches the blade between his two palms. Lutao take's deep breathe and leans his body on his sword pushing down on the blade, cutting Gori's palm as the blood drips, making it easier for the blade to move downward. Lutao pushes downward even harder, as the blade slowly moves even closer. Gori, now eye to eye with the point of the blade as

Lutao said: "I'm not like you I don't care how you die, as long as you are dead." The point of the blade is just a fraction of an inch from Gori's right eye, as the blood drips onto his face. Then in a split second Gori shift his body to his right and the blade plunges into the soil. He then kicks Lutao leading leg with his left foot, then he quickly shifts his body to his left and with his right heel, he kicks Lutao to the face. Knocking Lutao off his attack, as Gori gets off the ground. The rain slowly came to a stop, as Lutao looks at Gori and gives him an evil smile, to see Gori standing there without his sword. Gori gets into a fighting stance and said: "Even without my sword, this is the closest you will ever get, in killing me."

GORI'S BATTLE WITH LUTAO

But this time Lutao now has the upper hand. Lutao laughs and said: "Without your sword, we shall see." Gori stares at Lutao and then he pans his eyes to see something shining on the right side of the road, as the sun slowly appears. Gori knows it's his sword and prepares himself to make his move. Lutao notice and stood ready to attack. A moment of silence, tension and heavy breathing fills the air. And within seconds Gori pulls out his darts from his left sleeves and threw them at Lutao as he leaps for his sword. It was an unexpected move for Lutao as he deflected both darts, then came charging after Gori with an overhead strike. Gori falls to the ground as he grabs his sword and roll's onto his back, holding his sword with his right hand as he blocks Lutao's strike. Gori then grabs the handle with both hands as Lutao strikes downward three more times. Right, left, right as Gori blocks all three strikes, while still on his back. Then he gives Lutao a left handed back fist to the face, as Lutao leans in too close with his last attempt. Picking himself off the ground with his sword in hand, Gori came charging at Lutao with a right hook, as he is holding his sword, grazing Lutao face with the tip of his blade, cutting him on the left side of his face. Lutao nervously steps back and wipes his face to see his own blood coming from another man sword. Gori looks at the tip of his blade and sees a small drip of blood. He looks at Lutao as the blood run down his face and said:

"Now you have a match." Lutao yells with avenges as he charges after Gori. And with every strike of his sword, Gori blocks and deflect Lutao's attacks. They begin to fight there way down the mountain, Swish" swish' as the blades cuts through the thickening air. Lutao swings his sword to his left then flips the blade and comes back to his right. Gori quickly ducks underneath as the blade passes by, cutting off the ends of his hair. As Gori ducks, he grabs a fist full of dirt with his left hand, and throws it into Lutao's eyes, as he was stepping inward with another attack. Gori blocks Lutao's incoming attack with an outward block to the right, then steps inward striking Lutao with a right elbow to the face, then comes back with his sword, slicing Lutao on his upper arm. Gori continues to spin around, and with his right leg, applies a reverse sweeping kick, taking Lutao to the ground. Without thought, Lutao rolls his body into Gori's legs, knocking him to the ground. Swords still in hand as they both grabbed each others arms, and begin to grapple. Each trying to take advantage of one another, as they are both on the ground struggling. Twisting and turning as they wrestle there way off the Takai Yama Path. They didn't notice as they slowly started to descend, then began to tumble downward on the side of the mountain. They could not hold on to each other, as they both try to stop from falling. Flipping downward as they both tumbled, hitting everything in there path.

Both, now helpless as the force of gravity pulls them downward as they are trying to use their swords to cut anything that's in their way, not knowing what awaits a head. At the bottom of the mountain edge, there's a six foot drop. Moments later: "AAAA!!!" As they both became air born shooting up to twelve feet high then landed on sand, on a beach, located on the side of the mountain. Everything is spinning, and still with their sword in hand. Both bruised and covered in dirt as they both could barely get up to continue there battle. Once again they both tried to get up and charged at each other, but they only went a few steps as they went different directions and drunkenly fell. Gori then uses his sword as a cane and plunges it into the sand, and uses it to get up. Tilting from side to side, he walks over to the shore then falls to his knees. He picks up a hand full of water and splashes it on his face. Lutao drunkenly watches Gori, and seconds later he also did the same. They are reclaiming their mental balance, Gori gets up as the waves ran along the shore line, he get into position as he focuses on Lutao and said: "Here is where you die." Lutao quickly stands up, his face dripping with water as he almost trips over his own foot. He gets into position as he puts the tip of his blade in the water and digs it into the sand. He stares at Gori and replies: "Just like I took pleasure in killing your wife, I will also take pleasure in killing you." Gori focuses, and see Lutao intention once again; all of his aversion grew inside. At that moment Lutao brushed his sword upward from the ocean waters, using it as a shield as he attacks with an underhand strike up the middle. Gori side steps and blocks it with a outward block and deflexed Lutao sword to the left, Lutao then came around with an overhead strike from the left as Gori also blocks its. Then he strikes from the right then the left, also blocked by Gori. With the sword in his right hand, Lutao comes around with a wide swing as Gori ducks and blocks it upward. Lutao then spins around with his sword and comes down the middle that way also blocked by the shear mastery of Yoshima. The battle is now unfolding as it is nearing its final moments, as these two warriors fight they're way into the ocean waters. They are in three feet as Lutao notice he had no chance. So he slowly begins to head back to the shore. Gori know test that Lutao is now retreating so he keep on pressuring him. He attacks Lutao with a high strike to his left, then two low strikes to the right and left, then quickly strike upward to the right. Lutao blocks all four attacks as he is walking backward, heading towards the shore. Gori once again repeat the same attack, high left then low right as Lutao blocks them, low left then high right, but this time as Lutao blocks Gori attack, Gori applies a rotating motion with his sword and sweeps his sword away, as it lands point first on the sand. Lutao now seems afraid without his sword as he quickly turns and runs for it. The water made it hard for both men to quickly move, but Gori is right behind him, as he raises his sword and slices Lutao on his back.

GORI'S BATTLE WITH LUTAO

AAAA!!!! As Lutao keeps running towards the shore, and the waves making it harder for him to move. But he made it to the shore and is now nearing his sword, Gori right behind him. Lutao desperately leaps as he grabs his sword and rolls on the sand, and without much time in his hands, he turns around on one knee and blocks upward as Gori came's down with an overhead strike. "Ching" as the blades vibrate and Gori pushes down on the blades as it is getting closer to Lutao's head. Gori stares into Lutao's eye as he sees the sand of sweat rolls off his face. Lutao can smell the scent of his own death approaching. Gori breathing out as he pushes downward onto his sword even harder as the tip of the blade nicks Lutao on top of his head. And at that moment Gori felt a slight shift on Lutao sword and in one quick motion, Gori pulls back and came downward with a low strike. Lutao sees the shine of the blade, as it seems to be coming down in slow motion, and within seconds, cutting off his leading leg.

GORI'S BATTLE WITH LUTAO

AAAA! As Lutao yells as he grovels in the pain and fell to the ground. Lutao holds his leg as he is trying to stop his own blood from gushing out. Lutaos leg decapitated as he rolls over onto his stomach and raises his head by using his arms. Water and sweat drips from his face as he leans forward. Facing down at the wet sand, he grinds his teeth from the pain and asks Gori: "As a samurai, kill me!" Gori filled with rage stood over Lutao and replied: "Why is it… when a man is near his death they are always in search for honor." Lutao looks up at him as Gori continues: "Lutao… your head is the last thing I will be cutting off." Lutao rapidly breathing in and out as he prepares himself to attack AAAA! As Lutao leaps and try's to grab onto Gori. Gori showing no remorse steps back with his left foot as he pivots his body and raising his sword up and around, cuts off both of Lutao's arms. Lutao with the look of disbelief could not believe as he sees his arms fly through the air and falls to the ground. He cries in pain as Gori steps back to watch him grovel. Moments later Gori kneels down, looks at Lutao and said: "On that day you looked into my eyes and showed no mercy and no remorse when you killed my family." He grabs Lutao and pulls him up by his hair, stares into his eyes as he tells him: "So why should I." And plunge the blade of his sword into Lutao neck. Lutao's eyes widen as he begins to drown in his own blood. Gori gets up, leaving his sword injected into Lutao's neck, he walks over and picks up Lutao's sword. He grips the handle and aims the blade Lutao as the blood gushes out of neck and pours down his body. Gori looks into Lutao's eyes and said: "I told you I'll kill you where you stand." He raises the sword back as Lutao look at him and continues to say: "Killing you slowly was for my family and that is what you deserve." Gori eyes widen with anger as he swung the steal blade downward. "Shing" As he cuts off the head of Lutao with his own sword. The blood of Lutao sprays into the air as Gori stares at his decapitated body, as it twitches on the ground into lifelessness and said to himself: "A dishonorable death is what you deserve" and tosses his sword next to his body.

THE BE HEADING

He picks up his sword and takes a few steps back. He nears the shore as he drops to his knees and splashes water on his face. He shows a sign of relief as his looks out into the horizon. The sky appears red as the sun begins to set and the waves crashing as it washes up on to the shore line. He looks down and put his hands on his knees, closes his eyes and takes a deep breath. Gori then hears a sound and he grabs his sword tight as he slowly opens his eyes. He quickly turns his head to see his friend Pinattsu standing there. Gori smiles with another sign of relief as he pushes the blade back into its case. The horse nods his head as to say the same. Gori looks at him and said: "Its time… to go home, my friend".

Scene 15
Returning Home

It's a dark night as the moon hovers over the earth. Gori crosses the mountains as he is heading home. Hours later, an image appears from the distance. Nearly arriving as the sun begins to rise. As he nearing his home he envisioned his family waiting for his arrival. Then the sky breaks through as the sun shines on the earth, stretching across the rice field, as it begins to shine on his home. Gori stops and gets off his horse and walks the rest of the way. He then walks to where it all began; he looks to where his family now rests, where there is now a beautiful garden. Colorful flowers and a small lotus tree giving life to all that surrounds it. Without a word, he walks up to the tree and ties the strip of cloth that is now covered in blood around a small branch. He smiles with joy, but with sadness in his eyes. He kneels down in front of the tree and look up to the heavens, tears filled his eyes as it drips down his face. He softly inhaled as he places his hand on the tree, and bows his head and prays to his family: "My love, it is done. You may now rest in peace. Kiss the kid for me, I'll shall see you soon."

THE END

.OR IS IT?

Sixteen Century Japan and almost a year had past. The sky is gray as the day came with no sun. Only the smell of death fills the air. In a small village some where in Omi Japan, a man living in peace, by the code of the "BUSHI", and a new loyalty for life. On that morning he walks out of his home, as he prepares for his daily prayers, blessing the sky above and the flowers below as he kneels by a lotus tree. He bows his head to begin his prayer as he hears a sound, the sound of footsteps. He sense there's something wrong, he feels that he is being ambushed. Calmly he raises his head and begins to meditate. Moments into his meditation a voice yells out: "Yoshima GORI!!" Gori slowly opens his eyes and calmly said: "Whoever you are; you are standing on holy ground." The stranger grinds his teeth with anger as he replies: "You killed my brother, now I'm here to kill you!" Gori still at the meditating position bows his head and quietly said: "My love, once again our peace together is now over, please forgive me." He slowly gets off his knees and turns to the stranger and said: "Which

one of those bastards was your brother?"
The stranger could not believe his ears,
and quickly said: "I am Daimyo Takamuri,
the second commander of the imperial army
and all of the samurai classes. I am the
brother of the late SHOGUN, LUTAO! And now
it's your time to die!" Gori stands there
looking right at Takamuri and with only
a tanto on his right hip he replies': "If
this is the day I was meant to die, so be
it." Takamuri looks at Gori and points his
sword at him and yells: "GO!!!!" As an army
of a hundred or more dark soldiers came out
from hiding and attacked. Gori pulls out
his tanto and...

TO BE CONTINUED

GORI WITH SWORD AT HAND